I0744817
A cookie
and
cake
Holiday
JOSLIN FITZGERALD

Published by Circles Legacy Publishing LLC
Book design copyright © 2018.
Project Manager and Team Coordinator Mary Cindell Lynn Pilapil
Illustrations: Patrick Bucoy
Cover design: Norlan Balazo
Layout Coordinator: Vanz Edmar Mariano

Published in the United States of America

ISBN: xxx-x-xxxx-xxxx-x

Juvenile fiction / Fantasy and magic
Juvenile fiction / Family / General
November 21, 2018

Once-Upon-a-Time, there was a delightful pretty great space called Holiday-Place that was filled to the brim with sweet treats, cookies, cakes, gumdrops, lollipops, shakes, donuts, candy, pastries, jellies, and lovely Monthly glee! That means, the town was also full of snowflakes, sweet hearts, leprechauns, bunnies, flowers, rainbows, fireworks, ice-cream, pretty leafs, pumpkins, smiles, bright twinkling lights, likewise Pie!

So, stuffed with love, loaded up with many other lovely things, Holiday-Place was a great place to dance, live, and sing. That's why, full of cookies, cakes, ice cream, smiles and pie with everyone being nice day and night, as the delightful weeks were going up and down, Happy-Town.... was wonderful all year round!

Yes, indeed the people in neat Holiday-Place were all very Happy-Campers in every way, because Love, Life, also the amazing seasons were celebrated every-day! Next to make time nicer, also more sublime, as the months faded away dark to sunlight, things were cheerier, since all of the young and old, fun, huggable, mellow PEOPLE in Holiday-Place yearly Changed rotating Colors. And in that fun state they also Glowed... since they were all the colors of the rainbow!

So, in January their cute body shapes turned into a new cool winter's blue. In February the Happy-Campers were a great amazing shade of red through and through. In March they had green toes, and rosy cozy glows.

Next in April the Happy Campers showed up with purple noses. In May the gleeful people switched into a deep rich tint of pink each one looking just like a perfumed scented rose. Then in a delightful blink and wink of an eye, as nice June arrived, the glowing Happy-Campers changed into mellow yellow fellows.

Next in July, while fireworks lighted up the sky the friends turned red, white also blue. And as they looked like beautiful flags waving on the breeze that was very cool! In August the Happy-Campers traded places with the colors of the sea.

In September when fall was calling and the leaves were floating, they all had golden knees. In October everybody had orange cheeks. In November the young and old folks looked like rainbows with glows cozy and sweet. And last but not least, after changing into the colors of a pretty parade throughout the seasons, in merry December, the Happy-Campers were a neat picture of red and green.

Yes indeed in Happy-Town....as everything changed all year round, fading away nights and days were charming, colorful, sweet, and nifty! Therefore, as all the amazing, adorable Happy-Campers at Holiday-place were eating more yummy cookies, candy, also tasty-cakes, there was something fine to celebrate all the time.

So playing where gliding butterflies soared through the icy nighttime sky, and where the paint from a rainbow daily defined life, Holiday-Place was a nice Out-of-Sight-Land to hang around. Yes it was untold happiness living where no matter your age, everyone smiled, and no pouts, doubts, or grouches were allowed behind the happy gates!

To that lovely beginning things were even sweeter, because dwelling in that neat special Holiday-Place was a nice girl named Joy and kind boy called Toy who both experienced joy and adored playing with more toys. That means, enjoying their toys, while adoring their joy, the years in Holiday place were happily the same. So, knowing nothing could ever change their bliss, as the last season was over and done, loving the monthly parties everyone who lived in town, looked forward to the great fun coming around, as January's crowning snowflakes tumbled down.

That's why, as the cute New-Year-Baby arrived smiling, not crying, the kids liked playing in the pretty cold, blowing whiteouts, building people out of snow. And as they gleefully counted time down, all blue Happy-Campers enjoyed the delightful fireworks popping high above their heads, as night turned into daylight over their beds.

So, seeing the pretty wintertime fireworks showering their smiling snowmen in sublime starlight, while listening to the bright silver bells ringing in a new, new year, living in Holiday-place time was very nice, because laughter always filled the air. Yes indeed, as the clock stopped and started again there was no better safe space to be living in, since along the way evening turned into a cool New-Year's-Day!

That's when, Joy said "watching the sky change into a bright rainbow's light will always be a delightful way to celebrate time flying by." Nobody was surprised when kind Toy replied. "Knowing every-day will always be a holiday in life, I love watching the mighty firecrackers lighting up the wintertime sky."

So as the charming months passed by everybody was happy, because right after January said "Goodbye" February replied "Hi." Therefore opening up the New Year's door, as the flipping calendar started to turn its Re-running Pages one by one then and before, the changing red skinned kids, loved the following new cool tinted month full of candy, cookies, cakes, lollipops, gumdrops, and fun!

That means, the neat sweet Happy-Campers cherished Valentine's Day, since all you ever heard at work or play was, "I Love You, You're Wonderful, and eat more ice-cream, candy, cookies, and cake!" So, no surprise night to day with everything in the delightful town dressed up in nice pink, red, and white, there was no better divine place to be all the time. That's why, when Joy said. "Toy, Won't You Be My Valentine?" Toy replied, "Joy I would love to be your Sweet Heart Friend for life!"

I ♥ u
FLOW
you're wonderful
YOU,'RE SPECIAL

So everybody was happy as the old months passed by, because right after February said "Goodbye," March replied "Hi." And greeting March was also nice since all of the Happy-Campers celebrated another new great holiday called St. Patrick's Day! Yes that time was groovy for everyone, since that month was filled up with leprechauns, magic, rainbows, candy, ice cream, cookies, cakes and a warm sun.

That means, St. Patrick's Day was the introduction to a magical springtime full of sweet fun. Because, about the time neat St. Patrick's Day rolled around to play and sing, the pretty grass and Happy-Campers started to turn bright green. And as the green trees were budding, the pretty beginning of flowers started to be seen.

Therefore when Joy said "I love looking for the lucky sweet treats in the bright sun light." Toy replied. "I also like eating cookies and cake chasing the rainbows, while playing with the leprechauns in the park, running all around town sunlight to dark."

So everybody was happy as the neat months passed by, because right after March said "Goodbye," April replied "Hi." And thinking about the fun surrounding their candy eggs, bunnies, pastries, cookies, cakes, and treats, that repeating season was likewise sweet. That's why, as the Happy-campers turned into deep bright shades of violet and blue, showing off their cute purple noses too, it was not surprising when Joy sighed. "With all of the beautiful colors in life, while enjoying our sweet daily delights, there will always be a lot of nice sides to the sun arising." And agreeing with her nobody was surprised, when Toy replied. "Yes, Easter will forever be divine."

So as pretty spring was just starting to peek through the greening trees, as the Happy-Campers were turning new lovely shades of pink for all their friends and family to see, the cold months passed by. Because after April said "Goodbye," May replied "Hi." Yes, May was likewise a very special time at Holiday-Place, since the Happy-Campers loved to play in the parks, singing with their darling mother's morning to dark. Therefore, when Joy said "I love dancing around the May pole giving Momma pretty sweet flowers for her Mother's day." Toy stated "I also like giving my amazing Mama roses, donuts, treats, shakes, pastries, lollipops, gumdrops, Cookies and Cake!"

So, everybody was happy as the warming up months passed by, because after May said "Goodbye," June replied "Hi." Therefore all of the Happy-Campers loved changing into mellow yellow fellows. And everyone also adored welcoming in the sizzling summer days after class, as they played the new cool watery games and happily celebrated their Gladness. That means, June was a great time for the pleased children to run, laugh, play, sing and shout when the last bell rang out!

And since school was closed, getting out of tests, with no more messy homework stress, playing games in the green trees, spending time with their daddies, that made lazy June amazing. That's why, when Joy said "I adore Father's-day, likewise swimming in our wavy lake." Toy replied. "And I also love the hot high windy days going into July, since the changing weather makes the rainbows light up the sky."

SCHOOL
CLOSED

So everybody was happy as the months passed by, because after June said "Goodbye," July replied "Hi." And as everybody was changing into their colors of red, white, and blue, everyone at Holiday-Place loved July too. Because fiery July was an amazing time to take vacations, while celebrating freedom with nice fireworks, eating cheese, also corn-on-the-cob, fried chicken, peaches, apple pie, and baked beans. That means, proudly waving the flag high over her head every day when Joy said "In summer I love vacations and being free." It was not surprising when Toy replied. "Hot or cold any sweet season in our grand land is fine with me!"

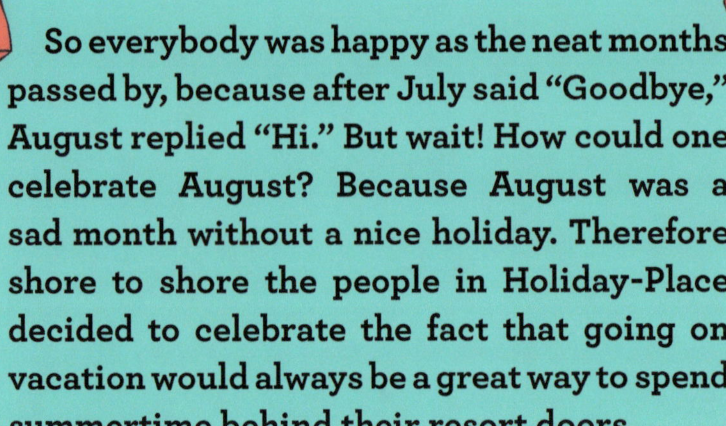

So everybody was happy as the neat months passed by, because after July said "Goodbye," August replied "Hi." But wait! How could one celebrate August? Because August was a sad month without a nice holiday. Therefore shore to shore the people in Holiday-Place decided to celebrate the fact that going on vacation would always be a great way to spend summertime behind their resort doors.

That means, as the Happy-Campers were turning into the turquoise colors of the sea, playing around lakes, eating watermelons, also daily swinging in hammocks rocked by lazy ocean breezes, everywhere you looked the nice people in Happy-Town were Smiling!

Next celebrating the neat holiday in August was additionally fun and easy, since after summer the children were happy to go back to school. Hence when Joy said "I love spending summer with family and friends, while dreaming about cool breezes, palm trees, and friendly soft calling summer winds." Toy replied "And after hot summer goes around the bend, I like going back to school again. Because I like finding out how smart I am by taking tests, studying hard, ending lesson stress, and finishing classroom mess. So knowing how great life will always be, that makes August groovy, also school and summer Cool, for everybody!"

So everybody was happy as the hot months passed by, because after nice August said "Goodbye," September replied "Hi." That means, as young and old were turning into the gorgeous glowing, pretty gold colors of fall showing off their gleaming knees over all, everybody in happy Holiday-Place also liked Labor-Day so they could sleep late.

That's why, taking a great break from work after stopping their odd jobs, and getting yet another cool holiday rest from school, the Happy-Campers in town, truly loved to play, sing, also shout out loud too. Yes, they loved dancing in then out of the flying fall leaves, each one lightly waving around like the tiny shiny rainbows leaving the sleepy trees. So, when Joy said. "I love every nice season as they arrive, then fade away." Toy replied. "At Holiday Place, any time will always be great."

So everybody was happy as the nice months passed by, because right after September said "Goodbye," October replied "Hi." And everybody loved October, since October was really chilly and sweetly thrilling. That means, as the Happy-Campers were turning orange, even with their teeth chattering, and cheeks freezing, they were having glee carving holes into cold sweet jack-o-lanterns that they could eat.

That's why, looking forward to the delightful pie later on that night it was a lot of fun lighting the candles inside the hollow pumpkins one by one. And as, the gleaming beams made pretty pleasing shadows on the swaying leafy trees, that was also tons fun. So, turning heart shaped food into works of art that looked like the moons cute holiday face... Kooky-Spooky-Halloween was always great.

Yes indeed, dressing up, while playing make believe running around on the nice sidewalks, while safely crossing busy streets, everyone loved being goofy and silly during Halloween. Therefore, when Joy said "After carving the pumpkins, I like playing dress up, going door to door saying Trick or Treat, and getting yummy cakes, cookies, candy, also sweet gumdrops, lollipops, pastries also neat treats.... with no unkind or mean icky tricks seen." Toy sweetly replied. "I agree, because Halloween's another fun delightful holiday, especially at night it seems."

So everybody was happy as more of the old months arrived. Because right after October said "Good-bye," cold November replied "Hi." And as the rolling snow was blowing in again, while all the Happy-Campers were turning rainbow colors showing off red noses, bow ties, and hair bows, everyone loved the beginning of the repeating winter season while greeting in Thanksgiving. That's why, as time was flying by, everybody was looking forward to turkey and a whole lot more pie!

Because, as nice Thanksgiving arrived it was time to eat a neat feast! That means, as they gathered together at the amazing Grateful-Table being thankful for everything, the young and old enjoyed their beets, meats, cranberries, stuffing, salads, chips, dips, pies, jellies, and other pleasing mouthwatering treats. Yes indeed. Thanksgiving was sweet and really tasty.

Therefore, happily dining while peacefully eating behind their delightful doors when Joy said "I love everything!" Nobody was surprised now or before when Toy replied. "Families, love, memories, food, pie, cake, and safe places, will always make us celebrate life, night and day."

So everybody was happy as the delightful months passed by, because right after nice November said "Good-bye," kind December replied "Hi." And in that nice, wise, exciting reply snowy December was another glorious time in life for the tall and small. Because the young also old, were likewise waiting for more sweets, neat treats, cookies, jelly, cakes pies, toys, candy-canes, gumdrops, shakes, lollipops, games, donuts, loads of icing, tasty pastries, also Mr. HO-HO-HO and his nice reindeer to arrive from the North-Pole.

Yes that merry season was the Happiest-Holiday around, since everyone was waiting for kind jolly Santa-Claus to come to town. So turning bright red and green, like the shops on the towns street, when Joy said "I love watching for the neat elves, reindeer, and nice sleigh to glide by and see me!" It was not surprising when Toy replied. "Waiting for Santa to arrive and fill our stockings with sweets, lollipops, gumdrops, cookies, candy, pastries, games, toys and treats also likewise more amazing books by our favorite author Joslin Fitzgerald...I know that divine joyful night, will always be the greatest time, for all nice girls and kind boys."

JOSLIN

Then Joy replied. "And getting cool presents including the new, new, sweet Joslin-Fitzgerald story called "A FUNNY FLUFFY PUPPY" that neat book will let us find out what happens when a funny, fluffy, puppy runs away, since she will not learn, listen, or obey. Because as the puppy thinks come means wait, sit means chase, jump means play, and stay means run away, I can't wait to see what fun lessons come her way as she ends up on Santa's sleigh Going Up, UP and AWAY!

Then Toy replied. And reading the other new coming soon Joslin story book called A Mermaid and A Sailfish Tail that's all about whales, sails, tales, and fish tails, while finding out friends who Bail you out of tight places, will always come in all sizes, ages, races, faiths, grades, shapes, also looks on their faces. That cute story, about doing things a new way, will be another whale of a tale any day!

Therefore, as the old exciting calendar rolled away as time likewise passed on by, eating sweet cookies, treats, ice-cream, candy, pasties, lollipops, donuts, icing, gumdrops, tasty cakes, and delightful yummy pies, looking forward to their new Mary Fitzgerald Joslin books to arrive, everything was great all the time! That's why, waiting for nice Santa to arrive, while making their endless Christmas wish lists day to night, things in nice Holiday-Place were amazing sunrise to moon-light!

funny
funny funny
funny
funny
puppy

Therefore with everything being a Holiday, while wearing only smiles on their faces their fine Happy Camper life was delightful! Yes time was wonderful!

Ok WAIT! Things were nice day to night, all of the time, moonlight to star-shine... UNTIL, All-of-a-Sudden something Sad, Angry, Un-glad, Mad, and Unkind, happened in Joy's life she could not face or hide! Bottom line. Something heart breaking and upsetting ended their smiles. That means, something BAD arrived!

And in that clue, breaking the strict town rules that said. "After you get out of bed Never tell or ever share anything mean, gloomy, doomed, crazy, sick, scary, fearful, tearful, harmful, or cruel that happens to you after the sun turns red," Joy ignored those warnings. Tragically, Joy started talking and squawking instead!

No, unhappy frightened Joy was not listening to what the Happy-Campers, guiding life pie providers, great Cake-Police, or smart nice Cookie-Security-Team said! Therefore with things changing over night right after getting out of her bed Joy, started Crying and Weeping. Joy was also SCREECHING, YELLING, SHEIEKING, AND SCREAMING!

So listening to that Creepy Racket everything Merry stopped in their Town! And hearing a Scary Crazy sound, never ever heard before, all the Happy-Campers who lived in Holiday-Place stopped celebrating, and next... Closed their Doors!

Sadly, that Chaos happened right after Joy broke the sweet Cake-Rules, as January started again. Because in review, as Joy told everybody she LOST her dear kitty-cat who was her next best friend, sharing that new gloomy news like she wasn't supposed to, a Life-Changing-Cloud-of-Frowns.... started to spread around town.

Because it seems, if just One Person was Unhappy, nobody could celebrate anything! Bottom line. With Bad, Mad, Sad things hanging about, with time going up also down, at the end of everything.... with everybody Pouting, Screaming, Screeching, Yelling, Shrieking and Shouting....nothing merry could, or would ever again, be found in Happy-Town!

So, with all of the Happy Campers life's and rainbows turned upside down, and their Skin Color flipped around with things being mixed up all out of whack...sadly everything happy, found in Town. changed after that sad, sad, sad, un-glad fact.

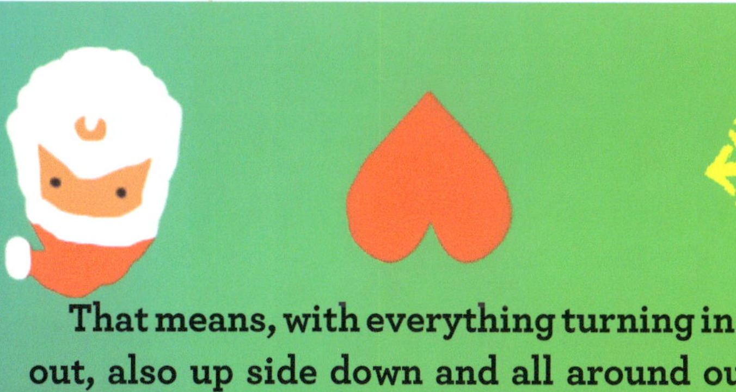

That means, with everything turning inside out, also up side down and all around out of whack... in January the Un-happy Campers were a whimpering orange. In February they were sad purple. In March they were gloomy blue through and through. In April they were a mad turquoise. In May they were a woeful yellow. In June they turned the slimy colors of the sea. That was something icky to see.

In July the pouting people wore tarnish gold. In August they looked like moldy old decaying wilting leaves. In September they were each something depressing mixed up in-between. In October they were a sick pink. In November they were striped icky red and white. And in creepy December, with all of the whimpering, sad, gloomy, mad, woeful, weeping, pouting, crying, teary, depressed, doleful, upset, mean, jumbled up colors of their rewinding minds showing on the outside, as young also old were changing their shades everyday with no seasonal symbol the same...like a moldy rainbow ....they did not look great!

So as the first tear-drop fell down nobody could bring happiness back to their stunned Holiday-Place. That means, a nice delightful, great, amazing, Happiness-Space that was once filled with colorful rainbow gladness, was brimming with sadness.

Then worse than that, after Losing kitty cat, with everyone breaking town rules by sharing their bad news, like they were not supposed to...all of the Happy-Campers in town were FROWNING! Because the families were remembering in the past, that they lost something cool, and somebody they also loved a lot too! So in that Angry, Mad, Un-glad state the whole confused town shut their Gates!

And as, everybody Changed into many odd Different Shades, and went into a new dark, deep, messy, sad place of distressed Agony, and Doom, nothing was the same at Holiday-Place, since Happy-Town was full of Gloom! Then tragically in that doomed upside down space there was nothing anyone could do, to change those days, because no blue skies of happiness or playful rainbows remained!

So it went night and day with everyone remembering, they were missing something or somebody they loved all the sadness attached to the fear, loss, and hurt never spoken of Escaped. That means, with some people losing their favorite toys no gladness remained. And worse yet with some families in the un-glad town losing their loved ones, as their faces changed, all joy, and grins were erased.

Following that painful growing, no longer hidden misery with other upset un-Happy-Campers missing beloved things including neat dreams, schemes, goldfish, lizards, dolls, balls, toys, games, birds, horses, goals, kitties, dogs, cars, homes, jobs, success, clothes, rings, hope, books, pots of gold, and more treasures missing....nobody was having any fun. So, with everything loved gone, including the sun... nothing was good for anyone!

That's why, the flag turned upside down! So, showing the town was in distress with no nice sweet dreams coming true, everybody was gloomy morning, night to noon. Because with some sad, mad upset people losing their Grandparents, Husbands, Wives, Friends, Brothers, Sisters, Mothers, others, dogs, cats, Fathers, Sons, Daughters, and with the very Un-happy-Campers misplacing sight, light, and time, the young also old around town were Whining, Shrieking, likewise Crying!

No, No-body was happy or smiling! And since that list of missing things and long lost people seemed endless, with all of the nice Happy-Campers also losing their minds, remembering the Mad-or-Un-glad times that already happened in their town, living in the Sad-Past the frowning folks who were not sleeping, decided to Wail and Weep! That means, with nobody sharing the painful hurt of what they dearly wished had never been... there were no more Happy-Campers living in town at years end.

So, with everybody turned upside down, everybody was crying. And with nobody smiling, also with Kitty-Cat still missing, it seems after losing the dream, at high cost of living in the odd bawling, sobbing tears of the past, the double-crossed-Lost-Holidays also could not last!

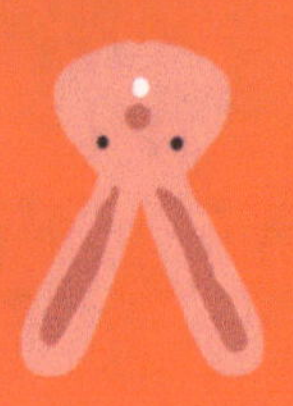

Therefore in review right after starting the New Year's gloomy season off too, with no wishes coming true, time stopped on the clock. And the fireworks would not pop. The snowflakes were hot. And the mirror dropped. Then when February rolled around, no more Valentines or sweet hearts were found in town. And with happiness lost everything was falling down.

Next when March rolled in nobody was playing games with their sweet friends. And since nothing was pretty or green everything stayed brown, grey, or something muddy mixed up in-between. Sadly, with nothing growing on the vine, spring was missing day and night. So when April arrived the frightened Bunny stayed inside.

Then when May rolled into play, with the high rising old winds blowing the flowers away, nothing was great after that day! Alas when June arrived calling, with no sunshine only hail and rain falling, the yelling kids were bawling. And since the rainbows were lost, with more storms popping up, all of the hot summer games, had to stop.

Next with the town still in distress when BOO HOO July flew by no one said anything about the hiding High-Flying-Fourth-of-July. Then when confused cold Snowy August appeared too, (since the unhappy kids were forced to stay in school all year through,) everybody was Un-glad, Sad, Mad, mean, unkind, also cruel. That means, being Un-Cool to friends, sadly beginning to end, with fun missing nobody was sure what to do.

So when September arrived, since no-one got a break after working all day, there was no rest, no sleep, no sweet-dreams, and no nice games to play. Next when gloomy October arrived nobody was wearing their costumes, since Kooky-Spooky-Halloween refused to say Boo. And worse happiness was lost too.

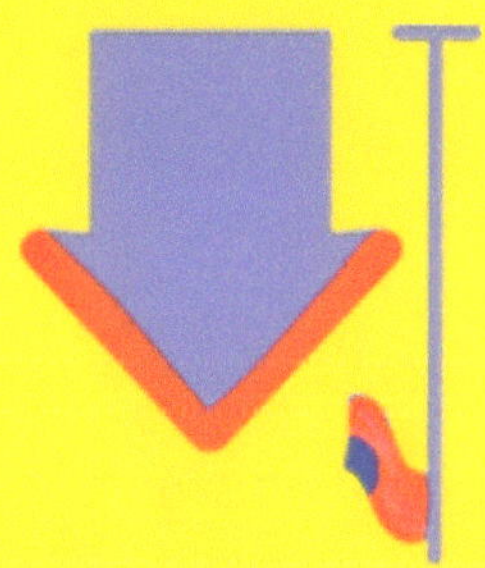

Then when Thanksgiving dropped by with the turkey, family, feast, and nice pie missing there was no reason to be thankful, since blessings were history. Next when it was Candy-Cane time, nobody danced around the wilting tree, because there were no sweet toys, cookies, or cake to be seen. And that dreary year, since the reindeers were not near every eye filled with tears, since Santa, Disappeared!

Bottom line. Sadly nothing was merry or right day or night, since everybody in town realized when something nice in life leaves, or tragically a loved one dies, in that sad Loss-of-The-Heart, always crying....there's no reason to celebrate holidays, or be happy about anything! Because there's only Rotten-Cheese-Misery remaining!

But WAIT! That's not the way things needed to be! Yes happily I have great news for everybody! Delightfully like a frowning rainbow learning to smile, things will always change in life! Because day to night nobody has to cry all of the time!

That means Screaming, Weeping, Wailing, Crying, and sadly Bawling going off track, with nothing bringing Kitty-Cat back, Joy realized even though her furry-Pal went away and others lost their sweet pets, Fathers, Mothers, Grandparents, Husbands, Wives, Friends, Sisters, Brothers, Sons, Daughters and Dreams in their work and play, that bad things did not have to stay that sad way. Because missing everything, including each person who took away great parts of their nice sweet hearts, forever and day, life could change, since something amazing remained!

Saying that everyone finally realized even though life, places, and faces will fade away, great pictures, and amazing stories of past glory, with sweet meaning memories always stay! And knowing as the seasons flip around things will get better day by day good times, new goals, growing happiness, also renewed hope will always be coming our way!

So after that great day, Joy and Toy finally understood sadness should stay in the past. And since nothing in the sad past will ever change anything that has already happened.... everybody likewise realized pain in the past... should also not last!

That means, sweet Inner Peace will NEVER depend on people or things who leave us behind. Because letting the sad, mad, past depart, January, February, March, April, May, June, July, August, September, October, November, and December all year long, happiness will remain and reside inside of our heart's awesome song!

So being fine with what we have right now, just like a frowning laughing rainbow that shows us, if you will just turn things around, everyone will realize there's two sides to life. Because for the young or old, happiness will forever be found in smiles, goals, also hope, in what happens today, tonight, and tomorrow!

And with that great new news found Joy also Toy, and all of the Un-happy-Campers in town agreed, their nice glee needed to come back around quickly! So, everyone in Holiday-Place realized, even though a lot of sweet, neat, kind things including kitties, doggies, goals, families, dreams, and friends, sadly one day will be missing, while going around the bend month after month, year after year the Un-Happy Campers needed to find a-way to laugh, play, grin and dry their tears.

So turning their frowns upside down like a glowing flipped over rainbow that makes the sky smile, the Now Happy-Campers found out without a doubt the nice presents of today, and kind gifts of tomorrow, will always be very great! Next, they realized if they were to ever open up their shut doors again to a new fun summer, fall, winter, or spring.... everybody would find, a new kind of growing forever love, and glowing Happily Ever After Gladness... only daily Hope cookies and cakes bring.

That means, the Happy-Campers needed a different peace beginning to the end, to chase away the grey fading days in their life. And to do that, the sad town realized that they needed to learn to Smile again! Because only a Grin and a new attitude toward cookies and cakes could bring great times back to Holiday-Place.

And with that great new news everything got better too. Because, knowing the missing names on our story's pages will always stay an amazing part of our heart forever, and best in life was yet to come along the way, the Happy-Campers realized living for today looking forward to tomorrow, joy will always remain!

That means, nobody was going to let the Last fear, past hurt, ending tear, or the final angry word said, that was following their awful painful loss all around town, break their hearts, or keep the doors closed in Happy-Town! Next finding a renewed fun way to sing, smile, laugh, grin, and play, everybody likewise realized no matter what happened yesterday, during the cold changing seasons for any old reason, today also tomorrow, that something new, and great was on its way!

Because, the gleeful HAPPY, HAPPY, HAPPY, HAPPY Campers finally realized if they would just look for the best in today that Happiness will always stay! Bottom line. The Happy Campers found out, no matter what thing, dream, or person left them behind crying, since the beautiful future starts a brand new day.... if they would just put their old sorrow and past draining pain away......that a Great, Happy-Beginning would always be coming their way!

Therefore in review of all the clues when sweet January, February, March, April, May, June, July, August, September, October, November, and hiding away December too, rolled back around again, everything in Happy-Town went from sad to Glad. Because, the Happy-Campers found out that turning their backs on unkind sadness, just by having Fun Right now....life and love, will always fill every day with Gladness. So knowing there will always be a way to be peaceful inside of your mind, the snowflakes, hearts, leprechauns, bunnies, flowers, rainbows, fireworks, divine ice-cream, pumpkins, pie, and pretty shiny bright lights made everything alright, all of their life. Because Happily Ever After.... was all the time!

Next enjoying the New Year full of cookies, candy, pie, icing, tasty cakes, gumdrops, shakes, lollipops, treats, and pastries, while drying their eyes night to day, the Happy-Camper's likewise realized their eternal grins and forevermore laughter would always make every great day amazing! That means, to mend a hurt heart, the smart Happy-Campers finally realized to enjoy life all the time, like a Frowning Upside Down Rainbow that flips around, TO STOP CRYING ALL YOU NEED TO DO IS SMILE!

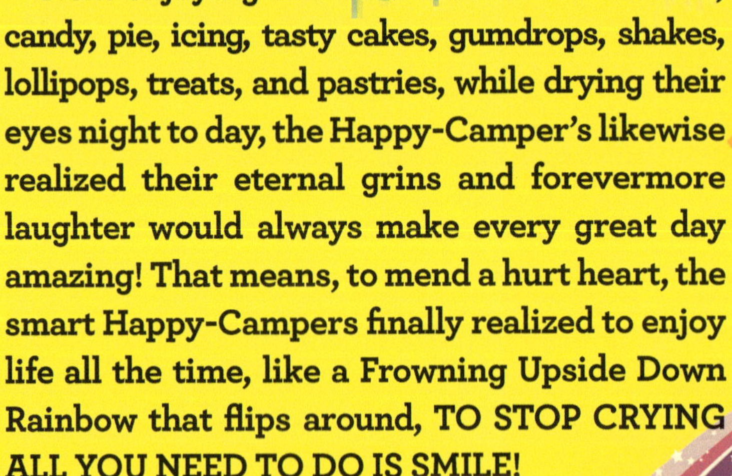
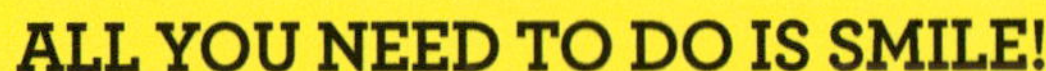

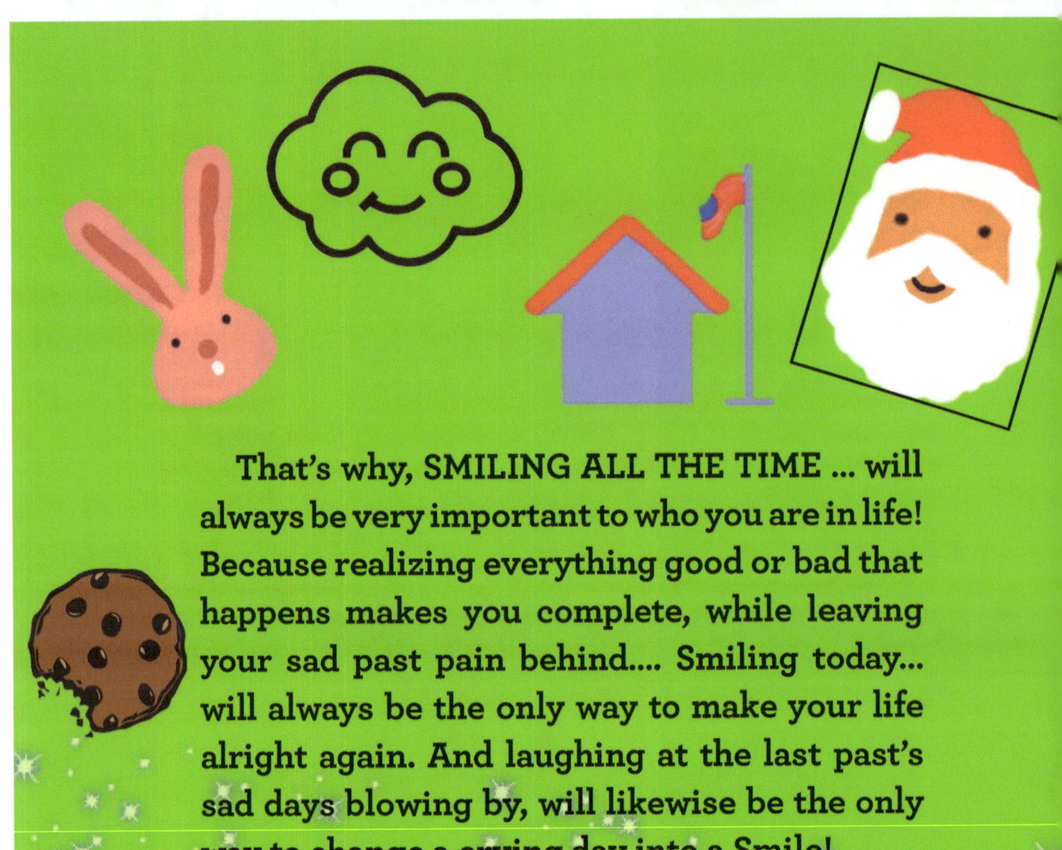

That's why, SMILING ALL THE TIME ... will always be very important to who you are in life! Because realizing everything good or bad that happens makes you complete, while leaving your sad past pain behind.... Smiling today... will always be the only way to make your life alright again. And laughing at the last past's sad days blowing by, will likewise be the only way to change a crying day into a Smile!

So, knowing pain, sadness and problems should never remain a part of your heart, the smart Happy-Campers found out having fun today going your nice way, will be the only way to remain happy every day! That means, being glad today, and happy tomorrow, will forever be better than living in the Past's sad sorrow! Because SMILING will always be better than crying!

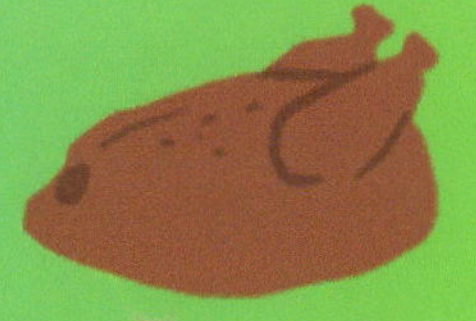

Bottom line. Everyone realized to make gladness last, closing a Tears-Door from the start will always be the most important part of a nice Happy-Heart!

So, stating that gleeful fact again Joy and Toy agreed.... if you will simply turn your doomed frown upside down into a delightful, nice Smile that looks like a kind rainbow's face, your heart breaks will change... Because when things get gloomy in your doomed mind, turning life and the days around....even when the hands of time, keep going up and down, everyone will find their own Happy-Town!

That means, always being Thankful for the sweet people in your life who are here, as well as being thankful for others who are far and near, while being grateful for what you have right now, sunset to sunrise, you will always be joyous all of the time! Therefore, every minute by closing your sad door night and day, even if a part of your heart goes away.... everyone will find the way to stay a nice Happy-Camper in every way. Bottom line. Enjoying time that remains....we will all find out, that no matter the season for any reason, if we will just QUIT CRYING AND START SMILING..... life will always remain a sweet Cookie and Cake Holiday!

So The-Moral-to-the-Story will always be the same today, tomorrow and or yesterday. Therefore, you need to realize, no-matter what happens in your life that makes you fearful, tearful, sad, hurt, doleful, angry, sick, un-glad, gloomy, lost, cry, scream, unhappy, weep, mad, worried, cruel, feel doomed, lost, or mean, since you Can Not change history...... you need to leave those unhappy, painful things, and scary feelings, behind you in the past, like your waking up from a bad dream.

That's why, finding a way to always be happy, just by leaving your unglad sadness behind that guiding smiling lesson.... will always be very important to your life! Because, daily finding peace with the way things are meant to be, while enjoying the neat sweet gifts found in the present, happiness will be all you will ever see.

Bottom line. By enjoying your nice arriving candy, gumdrops, lollipops, pie, treats, icing, likewise your amazing family, and kind friends who remain .....Everyone will find their Happily-Ever-After, today also tomorrow again and again. Bottom line one more time. No matter what happens as the world spins, even as people, pets, and things will be missing going around the bend if you stop crying and Keep Smiling, life will always be a Cake and Cookie Holiday ..... Beginning to THE END.

But wait dear friend that's never the end. And, since we are always looking for another happy beginning to start again, please join me in watching for my next cute children's book coming soon to a child near and dear to you called "A FUNNY FLUFFY PUPPY." And as we gather together let's find out what happens when a new funny, fluffy, puppy runs away, since she will not learn, listen, or obey. Because as the cute puppy thinks come means wait. Sit means chase. Jump means play. And stay means run away, stepping into some colorful paint, while turning many strange rainbow shades, I know you can't wait to see what silly fun adventures come her way. So, as she ends up on Santa's amazing sleigh Going Up, UP and AWAY, wanting to know how that funny fluffy puppy tale plays out, going along my Mary way, turning more pages.... I will see you again soon another day!

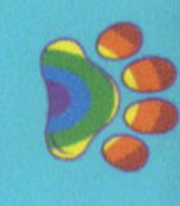

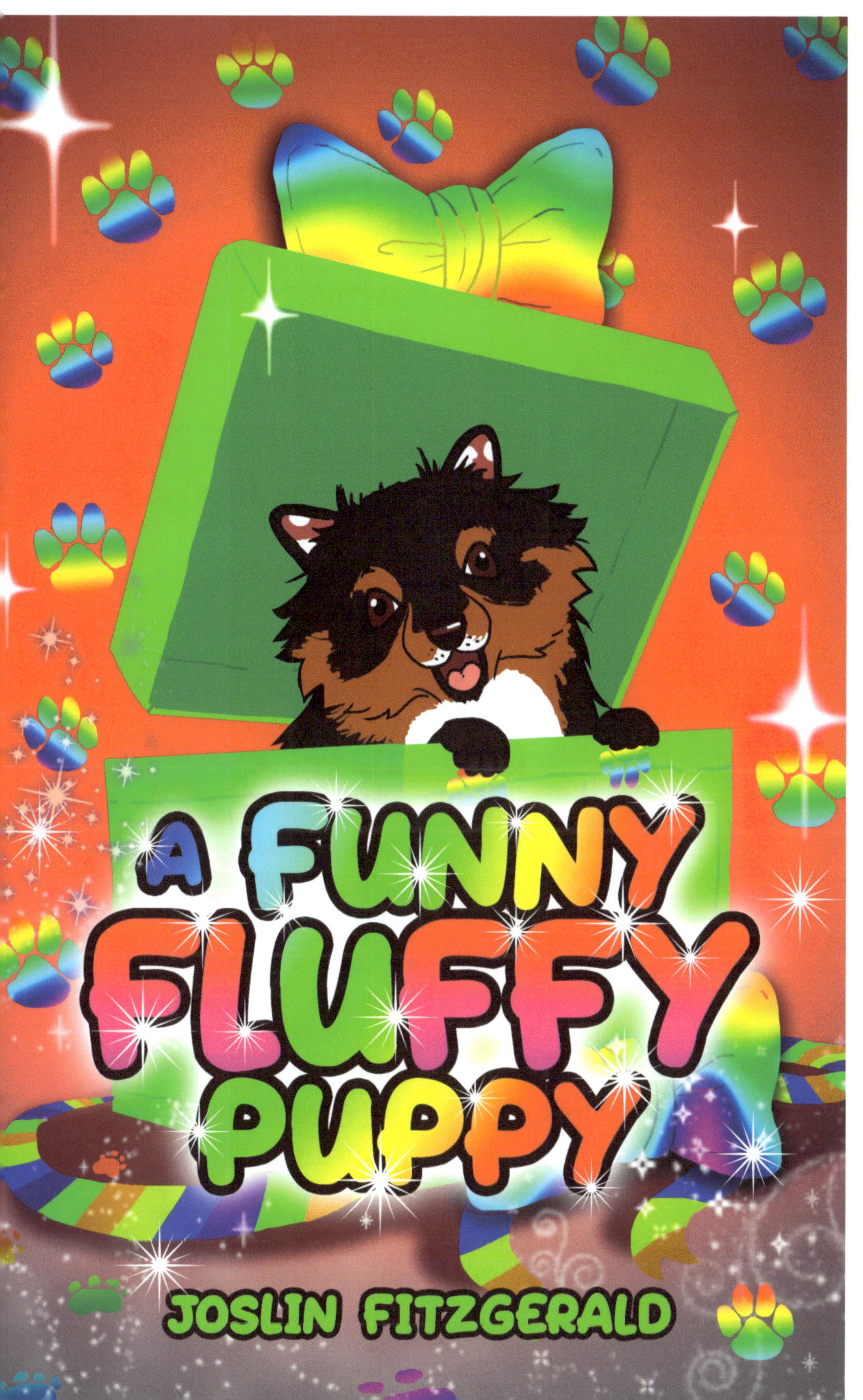

A FUNNY FLUFFY PUPPY
JOSLIN FITZGERALD

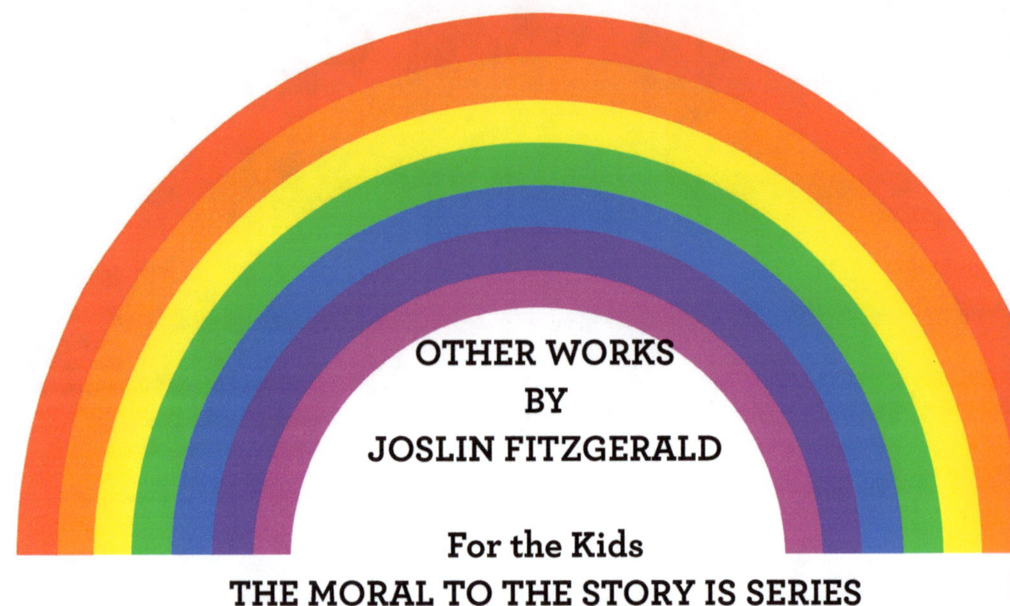

OTHER WORKS
BY
JOSLIN FITZGERALD

For the Kids
THE MORAL TO THE STORY IS SERIES

An Escaping Princess and
a Runaway Prince
A Kute Karing Kids Klub
A Neat Sweet Treats Dream
A Nice Wild Fairy Ride
A lot of Bugs and Teacups
A Small Star From Afar
At The Zoo Whos Whooo
All Frogs Sing Charming Songs
A Nerdy Humming-Birdie
A Cookie and Cake Holiday
And
COMING SOON
A FUNNY FLUFFY PUPPY too
AND FOR MORE INFORMATION ON
WHATS COMING NEXT
at your book stores,
Barnes and Noble also
Amazon.... please visit
www.joslinf.com